The Hare and the Tortoise

Jackie Walter and Andy Rowland

W
FRANKLIN WATTS
LONDON • SYDNEY

Once upon a time, there was a hare who was always showing off about how fast he could run.

Hare was always
teasing Tortoise.

"You're so slow!" Hare
laughed, jumping over
Tortoise, just to show how
much quicker he was.

Tortoise smiled at Hare.
"I may be slow, but I bet
I could beat you in a race,"
she said.

Hare could hardly believe his long ears. "There's no way you could beat me! I'm the fastest animal I know!" he spluttered.

7

Hare agreed to have a race the next morning. Hare and Tortoise woke up early and got ready.

"You'll never beat me!" laughed Hare.

"We'll soon see! Slow and steady can win a race just as well as speed!" smiled Tortoise.

Fox decided where the race would be run. He put up a start and a finish line. Tortoise and Hare would have to race once around the woods.

"Whoever crosses the finish line first will be the winner!" said Fox.

All the animals came to watch the race and cheer for Tortoise and Hare. Fox blew his horn and the race began!

GO Hare

Hare was sure that he would beat Tortoise.

"I'm tired after getting up so early," he thought. "I'll just have a nap before I start running about. I'll still have time to beat that slowcoach!"

He lay against a tree, closed his eyes and started to snore.

Tortoise crawled on, slow and steady. She didn't stop once. The day got warmer and she grew tired and thirsty, but on she crawled. She smiled as she passed Hare sleeping beneath the tree.

A few hours later, Tortoise slowly crawled across the finish line. Lots of animals cheered. But where was Hare?

19

Hare was still under the tree.
The sound of the animals
cheering woke him up from his
long sleep. He stretched slowly.

"Slowcoach Tortoise is
probably still at the start.
I can't even see her!"
he laughed to himself.

But Tortoise was just past the finish line. She was so tired that she quickly fell asleep with a big smile on her face.

"Time to run!" thought Hare. He raced to the finish line, grinning happily at the thought of beating Tortoise.

Hare was running so fast that
he didn't see Tortoise asleep.
He tripped over her and
went flying into the air.

"Tortoise is the winner!" cried Fox.

Hare could not believe it. "Well done,

Tortoise!" he puffed. "You were right.

You could beat me in a race

after all!"

About the story

The Hare and the Tortoise is a fable by Aesop. Aesop was a slave and a storyteller who is believed to have lived in ancient Greece between 620 and 560 BCE, making this story over 2,500 years old. There are many different versions, including a cartoon. A fable is a story that contains a lesson. This story might show that it does not pay to be boastful like Hare, or it might prove the proverb: "More haste, less speed." What do you think?

Be in the story!

Imagine you are Tortoise when Hare is teasing you. How do you feel?

Now imagine you are Hare at the end of the story. Are you sorry for teasing Tortoise before?

Franklin Watts
First published in Great Britain in 2015 by The Watts Publishing Group

Series Editor: Jackie Hamley
Series Advisor: Catherine Glavina
Series Designer: Cathryn Gilbert

A CIP catalogue record for this book is available
from the British Library.

The artwork for this story first appeared in
Tadpole Tales: The Hare and the Tortoise

ISBN 978 1 4451 4460 3 (hbk)
ISBN 978 1 4451 4462 7 (pbk)
ISBN 978 1 4451 4461 0 (library ebook)
ISBN 978 1 4451 4463 4 (ebook)

Printed in China

Franklin Watts
An imprint of
Hachette Children's Group
Part of The Watts Publishing Group
Carmelite House
50 Victoria Embankment
London EC4Y 0DZ

An Hachette UK Company
www.hachette.co.uk

www.franklinwatts.co.uk

FSC
www.fsc.org
MIX
Paper from
responsible sources
FSC® C104740